For Joyce, Ashifa and everyone
at Ottakar's Bromley
—A.M.

For Jazz
—J.T.

tiger tales
an imprint of ME Media, LLC
202 Old Ridgefield Road, Wilton, CT 06897
Published in the United States 2003
Originally published in Great Britain 2003
By Little Tiger Press
An imprint of Magi Publications
Text ©2003 Andrew Murray
Illustrations ©2003 Jack Tickle
CIP data is available
ISBN 1-58925-033-8
Printed in Belgium
1 3 5 7 9 10 8 6 4 2

The Very Sleepy Sloth

by

Andrew Murray

Illustrated by

Jack Tickle

tiger tales

Early one morning, deep
in the jungle, Sloth was
fast asleep.
But the rest of the
animals were wide awake.

Cheetah was on the treadmill, working on his

SPEED.

Elephant was lifting heavy weights, working on her

STRENGTH.

Kangaroo was
on the trampoline,
working on her

SPRING.

Monkey was
on the high bars,
working on his

SWING.

While Sloth stayed in
his hammock, working
on his sleep.
  "That Sloth is so lazy,"
said Cheetah.

"All he does is lie there!"
agreed Elephant.
  "Just dozing in his
hammock," added Kangaroo.

"Hey, Sloth!" called Monkey. "We're all working hard here. Why don't you get up and do something?"

Sloth slowly opened one eye. "Monkey," he said. "If you're so hard-working, you try lifting Elephant's weights."

"Easy!" said Monkey, and
he tried to lift the weights.
Elephant giggled as...

So Elephant tried to
jump on the trampoline.
Kangaroo shook her
head as . . .

So Kangaroo tried the treadmill.
Cheetah chuckled as Kangaroo landed . . .

So Cheetah climbed
the high bars and
swung right into...

By now, everyone was very hot,
very tired, and very, very cranky.
"This is useless," they muttered.
"Who caused all this trouble?"

"It wasn't me," said Cheetah.
"I was busy running."

"It wasn't me," said Kangaroo.
"I was busy bouncing."

"It wasn't me," said Elephant.
"I was busy lifting weights."

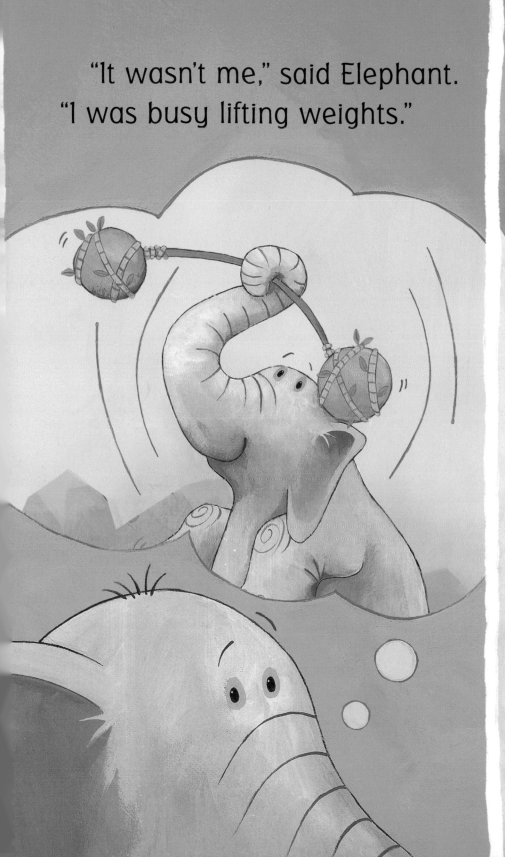

"And it wasn't me," said Monkey.
"I was busy swinging."
All the animals turned and looked at . . .

SLOTH!

"Hey Sloth," they called.
"You started all this!"

Sloth turned lazily. "You must see by now," he said. "We were all busy doing what we do best. Even me!"

The animals thought about it. "Yes!" they cried. "We're all good at running or jumping or lifting or swinging. But Sloth is the very best at . . ."

OZING!"

"Exactly!" said Sloth.
And with a stretch and a
yawn he fell fast asleep!